THE LITTLEST YAK

For my mum,
Who always sees the 'bigness' in me.
With all my love, LF xxx

For Jane and Helen – BIG THANKS! KH

SIMON & SCHUSTER
First published in Great Britain in 2020 by Simon & Schuster UK Ltd
1st Floor, 222 Gray's Inn Road, London WC1X 8HB

Text copyright © 2020 Sarah Louise Maclean
Illustrations copyright © 2020 Kate Hindley

The right of Sarah Louise Maclean and Kate Hindley to be identified as the author
and illustrator of this work has been asserted by them in accordance
with the Copyright, Designs and Patents Act, 1988

A CIP catalogue record for this book is available from
the British Library upon request

ISBN: 978-1-4711-8260-0 (HB)
ISBN: 978-1-4711-8261-7 (PB)
ISBN: 978-1-4711-8262-4 (eBook)

Printed in China
1 3 5 7 9 10 8 6 4 2

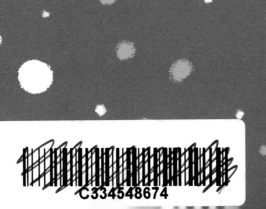

THE LITTLEST YAK

LU FRASER   KATE HINDLEY

SIMON & SCHUSTER

London New York Sydney Toronto New Delhi

On the tip of the top of a mountain all snowy,
Where the ice-swirling, toe-curling blizzards were blowy,

In a herd full of huddling yaks, big and small,
Lived Gertie . . .

the littlest yak of them all.

Now Gertie was GREAT at being a yak,
With the curliest, whirliest wool on her back.

She could clip-clop up cliffs,
no matter how slippy,

On little yak hooves that were splendidly grippy.

Yes, Gertie was all that a small yak should be

BUT . . .

... "There isn't," she sighed, "any BIGNESS in me!

I'm the yak at the back who is stuck in her smallness,
I want to grow UP and have greatness and tallness!
With the hugest of hooves and humongous horns, too,

There isn't a thing
that a BIG yak can't do!"

"But yaks," Mummy smiled, "are all shapes and sizes
And BIGNESS can come in all sorts of disguises!
Maybe one day you'll be huge, you'll be tall,
So don't rush to grow up when it's GREAT being small."

Yet as night tiptoed in and the stars filled the sky,
From the heart of the herd, Gertie sighed a huge sigh.

"Hugeness and tallness seem SO far away,
I don't want to be small! I need bigness TODAY!"

So Gertie began on a GROWING-UP PLAN

And ate every veggie a little yak can.

She pattered up mountains,
    she clattered down hills,

She hopped and she skipped

and she NEVER sat still!

And she read lots of books to make her thoughts grow
(Because grown-ups have big things
to think and to know).

And though Gertie hoped and she wished and she tried,
The days slipped away . . . but no growing arrived.

"What if," she sniffed,
"I'm a yak who CAN'T grow?"

And a salty tear plopped
from her cheek to the snow.

But wait! What was that?
Something was coming . . .

... A hundred yak hoof beats were steadily drumming!

And leading the herd in a snow-flakey flurry
Was Mummy Yak grunting, "Oh, Gertie! PLEASE HURRY!

Look up!
A yak's STUCK!
On the craggy cliff's edge!

At the end of the narrowest,
rockiest ledge!"

"OUR hooves are too heavy, OUR horns are too wide
To squeeeeeeze on a ledge on a steep mountainside!

But YOU are our littlest, grippiest yak.
Only YOU can squeeeeeeze up there and bring that yak back!"

"You need . . . ME?!" Gertie gasped,
"because I'm so . . . small?

My smallness can do something
BIG, after all!"

And Gertie was off.

There was no time to waste!

Over the ice-frosted rocks in great haste,

Up higher and higher,
leaping and springing,

Then onto the ledge where . . .

. . . a yak shape was clinging.

"OHHHHH!" Gertie squealed as she stopped in her tracks:
"Why, you're the tiniest . . .

weeniest . . .

TEENIEST OF YAKS!"

"I wanted to clip-clop up cliffs!" the yak shivered.
"But I'm not very grippy," and his teeny horns quivered.

"Well, gripping," smiled Gertie, "is what I do best!
Just hold on tightly . . . and I'll do the rest!"

So onto her back
the teeniest yak leapt,

And down through the
rocks and the ice Gertie swept . . .

. . . Home to the herd far below cheering loudly,
"GERTIE, YOU DID IT!" they all grunted proudly.

"The teeniest yak would be stuck, without YOU.
There are some things that ONLY A SMALL YAK CAN DO!"

Then Gertie was wrapped in a warm, woolly hug
And into her ear, Mummy whispered with love,

"As sure as the stars in the glittering sky,
You'll be all grown-up in the blink of an eye!

But it's here and it's now, whilst you're wonderfully small,
That you've found you've got bigness inside, after all."

And as Gertie gazed up at the moon's silver light,
"Being small," the little yak smiled, "is . . . all right!

For I'm just the right size that a Gertie should be.

I am perfectly little . . .

". . . and perfectly me."